ARNICA
THE DUCK PRINCESS

ERVIN LÁZÀR

ARNICA

THE DUCK PRINCESS

Illustrated by Jacqueline Molnár
Translated by Anna Bentley

PUSHKIN CHILDREN'S

Pushkin Press
71–75 Shelton Street
London WC2H 9JQ

Original text © The Estate of Ervin Lázár, 1981
English translation © Anna Bentley, 2019
Illustrations © Jacqueline Molnár 2014

Arnica the Duck Princess was first published as *Szegény Dzsoni és Árnika* in Budapest, 1981

First published by Pushkin Press in 2019

The translation of the book was subsidized by the Hungarian Books
& Translations Office of the Petőfi Literary Museum

1 3 5 7 9 8 6 4 2

ISBN 13: 978-1-78269-220-1

Designed and typeset by Tetragon, London
Printed and bound in Italy by Printer Trento SRL

www.pushkinpress.com

CHAPTER ONE

*In which we team up to write a story and
get to know the main characters*

"Write me a story!"
"What about?"
"The duck king and the duck princess."
"About two ducks?"
"They're not really ducks, you know."
"What are they then?"
"They're really a proper king and a proper princess. It's just that the wicked witch has cast a spell on them."
"Why has she done that?"
"Because of Poor Johnny."
"Johnny sounds like an English name—is he English?"
"Of course he isn't! Poor Johnny is Poor Johnny and that's that. He's got nothing except the shirt on his back and wanders about wherever he wants, whistling as he goes."
"And why was it because of Poor Johnny that the witch turned the king and the princess into ducks?"
"She didn't want him to marry Arnica."

"And who's Arnica?"

"The princess of course, who else would she be?"

"Ah, Princess Arnica! Who was so sweet and gentle, that when she smiled, wolves and bears forgot their fierceness. Even the wild wind became still. Everyone loved King Tirunt's daughter."

"King what?"

"King Tirunt. Isn't that what Arnica's father is called?"

"Oh, yes. That's his name. King Tirunt. Absolutely."

Far away, over the mountains and beyond the valleys, beyond the valleys and over the mountains there was once a round lake. By the side of the lake stood a royal palace with thirty-six towers and three hundred windows. In this palace lived King Tirunt and his daughter Arnica. The king was a very fair man. He punished those who needed punishing, and rewarded those who deserved a reward. But there was one thing that showed more clearly than anything else what a good king he was: he would never order anyone to do anything when he was in a temper. If he did lose his temper—and kings often do—he would retreat to his throne room, saying, "Now whatever I say, don't pay it any heed. Ooh, I'm angry! You'd best get out of my sight, you sons of dogs, before I tie you up by your heels! Get out, everyone, and count to a thousand. When you've done that, you may peek in and see if I've calmed down or not."

Well, everyone would scramble out of that throne room so fast that their feet barely touched the threadbare Persian rug! Standing outside, the Chief Royal Counter would quickly count to a thousand. Then the courtiers would peek in at the king, generally quite boldly as, by that time, his anger would have evaporated.

If it hadn't, then when he saw them peeking at him, the king would yell, "Out with you, dogs!"

In such cases, the Chief Royal Counter would count to another thousand. More often than not, at eight hundred and eighty-eight, the king would come out of the throne room and say:

"Sorry, everyone, if I called you dogs and sons of dogs, but I was like a mad dog myself."

But such two thousand—or one thousand, eight hundred and eighty-eight—scoring fits of rage were as rare as hen's teeth because King Tirunt was a wise man and his anger quickly passed.

"Where did it pass to?"

"Angerland."

"Is that where the Angers live?"

That's right, and they like to get into people's hearts. They're always on the lookout for one they can enter. And once the Angers have got into a person's heart, no amount of shaking and huffing and puffing and going red in the face will make any difference. That poor person can go on shouting till they burst!"

"Or until their Anger flies off back to Angerland."

"That's right. The sooner the better."

"And what if someone wandered into Angerland by mistake?"

"Then woe betide them, woe and weeping and wailing a thousand times over!"

"Why? Is there no such thing as good anger then?"

"Of course there is. Absolutely there is."

"And when King Tirunt got angry, was it good or bad?"

"Both good and bad. But I want to tell you about a time when his anger was good."

It happened once, and once only, that the poor Chief Royal Counter had to count so much his throat got quite dry. On that occasion, he had to count to five thousand. Hardly surprising, given what had happened. That would have made anyone angry, not just King Tirunt. One fine day two knights had turned up in the palace courtyard, their helmets flashing and gleaming in the sunshine, their armour rattling and clanking, and their horses blowing and stamping and pawing the ground. All this clattering, stamping and neighing brought the people of the palace, young and old, out into the courtyard. King Tirunt and Arnica came out too.

"And who might you be?" asked the king.

"Greetings to Your Majesty, the greatest of kings," said the knights. "And greetings to Princess Arnica, the most lovely, the most beautiful girl in the world."

"But I'm not the most lovely or the most beautiful girl in the world," whispered Arnica to her father.

"Doesn't matter," said the king. "One day there'll be someone for whom you'll be the most lovely and the most beautiful."

With that, he turned to the knights.

"What do you want?"

"We request your daughter's hand in marriage, Your Majesty," said the knights. "We realise of course, that she can marry only one of us. Therefore, we have decided that we will fight a duel to the death right here, in this courtyard, and whichever of us survives will have Arnica."

This was greeted with delight by the courtiers and the palace staff. A good little scrap was in the offing and they'd get to see it!

The two knights were already drawing their swords. However, both the rejoicing and the brandishing of weapons turned out to be a little premature.

"Stop right there!" said the king. "I'm not having a fight on my hands."

The knights lowered their swords and looked at the king.

"What do you mean? Don't you want to give us your daughter's hand in marriage?"

"It's not for me to decide who my daughter marries," said the king.

"Then who should decide?"

"My daughter. When she gets married, it'll be to someone she loves. And to someone who loves her. There's no point in you two hacking away at each other, if my daughter happens not to love the victor. And if she happened to love the vanquished one, well, that doesn't bear thinking about. Better forget the whole thing."

"You mean to say that your daughter wouldn't want to marry the victor?"

"I meant just what I said," said the king. "My daughter will marry someone she loves."

"And what if she happens to fall in love with some riff-raff?" asked the knights. "Some fly-by-night, some traveller-type, some empty-pockets, some sleep-in-the-straw?"

Red patches were appearing on the king's cheeks. To those in the know, it was clear that he was about to lose his temper.

"Then that fly-by-night, that traveller-type, that empty-pockets, that sleep-in-the-straw will be her husband," said the king, a touch louder than usual.

"Hardly proper for a king, that way of talking," said the knights snootily.

Now the king was shouting.

"Not proper for a king perhaps, but proper for a man! Take them to the prison and off with their heads, both of them!"

The Chief Royal Counter had already begun to count. One, two, three...

The king dashed into the throne room, pressed himself into the farthest corner of it and there he fumed and he huffed and he puffed. Anger had got into his heart all right.

The knights looked at the courtiers in dismay.

"Are you going to chop our heads off right now?"

"Of course not. Just get out of here as fast as your legs can carry you!" said the Chief Courtier.

The Chief Royal Counter had got to three hundred and thirty-three.

By the time he reached one thousand, the two knights couldn't be seen for dust.

The peekers had a peek in, but the king was still so enraged that he flung his crown at them. It took him till five thousand to calm down. Then he came out of the throne room and said:

"I rather fear that, while I was angry, I may have told you to chop off their heads. I do hope..."

"Not to worry, Your Majesty," said the Chief Courtier. "We didn't touch a hair of their heads. Let them run off, I say."

"Oh, thank the Lord!" said the king, much relieved. "What a pair of dunderheads! They're *just* the sort I'd give my daughter to. Eh, Arnica?"

Arnica smiled at her father, and said, "Thank you, dearest Father."

"Because Arnica is going to fall in love with Poor Johnny, isn't she?"
  "I reckon so."
  "Do tell me when Poor Johnny's going to come into the story!"
  "He's on his way. He's already in a wood nearby."

CHAPTER TWO

In which Poor Johnny, the most footloose and fancy-free of all people, grapples with the Witch of a Hundred Faces

There was Johnny, strolling through the middle of the wood. As he strolled along, he whistled a tune, sometimes a merry one, sometimes a mournful one, depending on what mood he happened to be in.

"I must be the poorest person in the whole world," he thought, and began to whistle a sad melody. And it was true, besides his staff and his pocket knife, he had nothing except the shirt on his back.

"But it also happens that I'm the richest person in the world," he thought, and in that moment his whistling became full of trills and turns. And, yes, he was the richest person in the world: he had the woods, the blue sky, the birds, and even the weeds growing by the roadside. All the great expanse of this wide world was his to enjoy.

Then, something else occurred to him that made his whistling yet more cheerful. "When I come to think of it, I'm also the most footloose and fancy-free person in the world. I can go wherever I want and when I get there I'm free to turn somersaults to my heart's content. No jumping to anyone's command for me! Hey, there's not a person in the world freer than I am!"

Then, becoming downhearted once again, the tune he was whistling turned sorrowful. He had realised that he was more of a prisoner than anyone in the world; that his freedom in fact held him in fetters. He had neither a friend nor a sweetheart, not even a hand's breadth of land to call home and on which he could lay down his head to sleep.

Well, there he was, whistling and thinking to himself as he strolled in the deep dark forest under the great arch of the sky and he was completely unaware that in doing this, he had strolled into our story. Neither did he know that he had strayed onto land belonging to the Witch of a Hundred Faces. If he had known where he was, he would most certainly have hotfooted it out of there. Not, we hope, on account of our story, but on account of the Witch of a Hundred Faces, whose wickedness and cunning had no match for many leagues around.

"Why was she called the Witch of a Hundred Faces?"

   "Because she could appear in a hundred different guises. She could turn herself into a dog or a bat, or even a wasp if she chose. And she could change her human appearance as easily as you or I change our socks. She could make herself look beautiful, or ugly, young or even old and wrinkly whenever she wanted."

   "It's not good to be a witch, is it?"

   "Why not?"

   "You have to make trouble for everyone and bring them sorrow. It must be awful."

The Witch of a Hundred Faces was sitting huddled and despondent by the door to her house. She was thinking that in the blink of an eye, the seven years would be up. For, every seven years, a witch has to make someone her slave. Not by force, but by trickery. If the person doesn't enter into it of their own free will, the arrangement won't be valid. With barely a year left of the seven she had, the witch still hadn't managed to hook another person to be her slave. The people of the area were all careful to give the wood a wide berth, precisely to avoid her, and strangers were not likely to wander that way, the forest being almost at the world's end. Thus it was that the witch could only weep and wail, "What will become of me if I lose my magic powers?"

Ah, but listen! The witch's eyes lit up. She could hear whistling.

"I'll be blowed if that isn't someone coming this way on the road through the woods," she said to herself. And she was right. Poor Johnny was on that road, getting nearer all the time. Ooh, the witch went mad with excitement!

"This one's mine," she thought. She set to and turned herself into an ancient, doddery little old lady, complete with a stick and a crutch to lean on. Just at that moment, Johnny reached her house.

"Oh, dear boy, what luck that you're here," said the witch. "You'll help a poor old lady, won't you?"

"Gladly. What can I do for you?" asked Poor Johnny.

"I'm not well at all. Can't hardly manage by myself these days," bluffed the witch. "Will you agree to work for me?"

"Well, Mother," said Poor Johnny, scratching his head. "I'm happy to help with whatever needs doing, but I can't agree to work for you. In case you didn't know, I'm the most footloose and fancy-free person in the world. I don't work for anyone."

Well, you should have seen the witch's face when she heard that. Of all the people to come wandering this way, it would have to be the world's most footloose and fancy-free one, the devil take him!

"You'll work for me, whoever you are!" she muttered under her breath. "Oh, it wouldn't be for a long time," she coaxed Poor Johnny. "Only three days. Three teeny-weeny little days. You'll see, they'll fly by so fast, you won't even notice them."

"No," said Poor Johnny, shaking his head," I won't work for anyone, not even for a half a minute."

"But I would pay you handsomely," persisted the witch.

Poor Johnny became curious.

"How much would you pay?"

"Come and see."

She led him to the door of her store cupboard and opened it. Poor Johnny had to shield his eyes with his arm, so bright was the light that poured out. The cupboard was full of treasure, gold coins, real pearls, silver and jewels all sparkling and gleaming. The Witch of a Hundred Faces blinked cunningly up at Poor Johnny.

"All yours," she said. "All you have to do is work for me for three days."

Now, what do you think the most footloose and fancy-free person in the world said to that?

"What the devil would I do with all those gewgaws?"

The witch could barely conceal her anger.

"You call these gewgaws, you halfwit, you dunderhead, you melon! These are handpicked treasures, not trinkets! Odds bod kins! The richest king in the world would dance for joy if he could have these for his treasury. Now... three days' work and they can all be yours."

Poor Johnny shook his head.

"And what would I do with all this treasure? I wouldn't be able to lift it for one thing. And say I could, I'd soon be worn out carrying it around. Not likely!"

"Dunce!" said the witch. "Buy yourself a horse and cart and load it onto that. Ride on the cart, and you won't even need to walk."

"Firstly, I like walking. Secondly, if I had a horse and cart, I'd be eaten up by worry. The horses would always need feeding and watering, there'd be all kinds of bother with the cart; new wheels, new brakes... Ah no, that's the last thing I want! Thirdly, what about robbers? I'd have to guard the horse, the cart and the treasure from them. Ha ha, I'd even forget to whistle. Keep your treasure, Mother. You're welcome to it."

"Oh, you're a worthless good for nothing," said the witch. "Bother with the horse and cart! You'd have servants. As for the robbers, you could build a castle to keep them out. You'd have more than enough money. A castle with good, thick walls, then no robber would be able to break in."

"So I'd be cowering in my castle for the rest of my days, is that it? All pasty and pinched looking? I wouldn't be able to go out for a nice walk, because I'd always be thinking, 'Oh no, what if my castle gets struck by lightning? Alas my castle this and alas my castle that!' I don't need your treasure, old Mother. But I'm very happy to help you out of the goodness of my heart. Just tell me what to do."

The witch fumed and pretended not to hear that Poor Johnny had freely offered his help.

"You'd have hardly anything to do in those three days," she spluttered. "Your only job each day would be to pick an apple for me from that tree."

In the yard stood an apple tree, a low, stunted thing, with exactly three apples on its branches. A child could easily have reached them all, without even having to climb up.

"Oh well, that's no trouble at all," said Poor Johnny. "I'll get them all down for you right now, for nothing."

He stepped towards the apple tree as he spoke.

The witch flung away her stick and her crutch and leapt to her feet as if a wasp had stung her.

"No, don't touch it!"

Poor Johnny looked at her distrustfully.

"Well, for a frail old woman you're mighty nimble all of sudden! Where are you a-limping off to?"

The witch had jumped up. Well, of course she had. As you might have suspected, this wasn't any ordinary apple tree. Every one of the poor people who had agreed to work for the Witch of a Hundred Faces had chuckled to themselves thinking what a small task they had to do to get a pile of treasure. After all, the three apples were so easy to pick, a small child could easily have done it. The first *was* easy to pick. Yes, of course, the first was. What none of them knew was that, on the second day, when they had to pick the second apple, the apple tree would grow so tall that, trying your hardest, you would need to climb from morning till noon to reach it, and from noon to evening to carry it down. Not to mention the third day. For on the third day, the tree would grow so tall, that, even if you were to grow wings on your back, you wouldn't be able to bring down the third apple before nightfall. Then the Witch of a Hundred Faces would step forward and say, "There'll be no treasure for you, and what's more, you can say goodbye to your freedom. You didn't complete the task, so you're mine now from top to toe!" I'm afraid so. And what could that poor person do? After all, they'd agreed to do the work.

"But Poor Johnny didn't agree to do it."

"No, he didn't. You heard what he said."

"He didn't belong to the witch, from top to toe."

"Not a hair of him belonged to the witch."

"He did the right thing to refuse the treasure, didn't he?"

"It certainly looks that way."

"And what if you'd wandered into the forest and ended up at the witch's house, would you have wanted the treasure?"

"Well, you know, it wouldn't have been so easy for me. I would have started thinking about all the things I could buy with that huge amount of money."

"Like what?"

"Like a talking doll for you, a big house near the woods and the lake, lots of clothes for you and your mother. We'd be able to replaster your grandfather's house and mend his fence too."

"But Poor Johnny didn't have to think about it at all, didn't you see? He just said no."

"It was easy for Poor Johnny. Of all the people in the world, he is the most footloose and fancy-free. He's got no one he needs to buy a talking doll for and he doesn't have a house that needs the fence redoing."

"But if you agreed to work for the witch, you'd be hers from top to toe."

"There's the rub, sadly."

"You know what?"

"What?"

"At the last minute, you'd notice something you didn't like about it and you wouldn't agree to work for her, OK?"

"OK. Fine by me. No way I'm working for her!"

"You see? I'd rather not have a talking doll, not ever. Poor Johnny just left the witch without a backward glance, didn't he?"

CHAPTER THREE

In which Poor Johnny suffers pains both in his legs and in his heart

T hat's right, Poor Johnny had left the witch without a backward glance, and faster than you could say "Jack Robinson". As for the thought that he'd most probably just met a witch, he brushed that aside as best he could and just ran for all he was worth. He hurried along, determined to put as much distance between himself and that house as possible.

The Witch of a Hundred Faces wasn't going to let her victim get away just like that, however. She first had to work herself up into a rage, then—hey presto!—she was racing through the forest in the shape of a storm, pulling up trees and stripping the grass from the ground. She buffeted and tore at Poor Johnny too.

"Blow this weather!" grumbled Poor Johnny, and kept on running. He'd weathered worse weather than this.

Before long, the witch had blown herself out.

"Now," she thought to herself, "I'll need to use my brain a bit if I'm to stop this layabout before he gets off my land." In no time she had contrived a plan. Giving herself a shake, she turned into an enormous shaggy-legged wolf. She gnashed her teeth and let out such a wonderfully successful howl that the whole forest trembled.

"Uh-oh, there are wolves coming!" thought Poor Johnny. "Come on, run for it!" He put on a spurt, but the wild howling seemed to be getting closer and closer, and from time to time he could even hear panting behind him. This was no joking matter, and he ran on just as fast as his legs could carry him. This was exactly what the old witch had been waiting for; quick as a flash, she changed herself into a tree stump right under Poor Johnny's feet. Whoops! Poor Johnny fell over so hard that the earth boomed under him. And, unfortunately, something also went "crack".

"My leg!" sighed Poor Johnny. Sure enough, he'd broken it. When he tried to get up, he found he couldn't. He had a shooting, burning pain in his leg and he heard more cracking. The Witch of a Hundred Faces had changed herself back into an old woman and was quickly smoothing down her hair.

"Right," she thought, "I'll go over to him and tell him that I'm going to heal him. I help him back into my house, and his lordship will never get out again, or my name isn't the Witch of a Hundred Faces!"

She made haste, because she could see that Poor Johnny was lying right on the boundary of her land. He was lying so that his broken leg was inside the boundary, while his body, his head and his arms were outside. Beyond the boundary, the witch was powerless. So she hurried along, hoping to tempt Poor Johnny back onto her land. If that didn't work, she could always drag him back over. Yet, when she looked up from smoothing down her hair and straightening her clothes, she saw that there was a girl crouching next to Poor Johnny.

"Odds bodkins!" the witch muttered angrily to herself. "Now what do I do?"

"Oh, your poor thing! You've broken your leg!" said the girl.

Poor Johnny was so surprised that, forgetting all about his leg, he sat up. And what luck that he did, for in sitting up he had shifted himself off the witch's land.

"W-w-well now, who are you?" he stammered. He had never seen such a beautiful girl in all his days. It wasn't so much that she was beautiful... more that he'd never in his life seen such a kind, gentle girl. Or rather so beautiful and so kind... Ooh! There was such a sharp pain in Poor Johnny's leg! And not only there; there was a sharp pain in his heart too.

The girl helped him up carefully and set off with him in the direction of her home.

"Just lean on me, don't worry," she said.

"Uh-uh," said Poor Johnny, shaking his head, "a great lump like me, I'll be too heavy for you."

"No, you won't," said the girl. "Come along. Does your leg really hurt?"

"That's pretty bad too," said Poor Johnny, "but whatever it is that's sticking into my back hurts much worse."

"That's funny," said the girl. "There's something sticking into mine too."

There was, of course. It was the witch's look as she watched them go. That's what they were feeling, like an iron fork in their backs.

"Just stop there, you two! Odds bodkins! I'll give you what for!" the witch was muttering in a helpless rage.

"The girl who's helping Poor Johnny, that's Arnica, isn't it?"

"Who else? She was out picking mushrooms in the forest, when she saw someone go 'whoops' and fall over. She realised he couldn't get up, so she ran over to help."

"And have they already fallen in love?"

"I think so. Both their hearts are really tingling. You heard that Poor Johnny was getting sharp pains in his."

"And people do fall in love quickly, don't they?"

"Well, some do, some don't. But it's not important how fast they fall in love. What matters is whether what they feel is true love."

"Is there such a thing as love that isn't true?"

"No, there's no such thing. Just sometimes two people think they love each other when they don't."

"But Arnica and Poor Johnny aren't one of those 'don'ts', are they?"

"We'll find out."

"How?"

"From what they do."

"What are they doing right now?"

Arnica took Poor Johnny back to the thirty-six-towered castle. She put a splint on his leg–she was really a very capable princess, you know–washed him and fed him and was happier than she'd ever been. The palace staff started whispering to each other, "Well now! What's happened to our Arnica? She's been pottering about so cheerfully ever since that man with the broken leg arrived."

Even Arnica was surprised at herself. "Well now! What's happened to me? How cheerfully I've been pottering about ever since that man with the broken leg arrived." King Tirunt, however, only smiled. He knew, after all, why Arnica was pottering about so cheerfully. She had, of course, fallen in love with Poor Johnny.

Poor Johnny moaned and groaned and complained indignantly– because of his leg, you might be thinking. You'd be wrong then. What did he care about his broken leg! It was his heart he was moaning and groaning and complaining about. It was jumping and wriggling like a gleeful young goat. It jumped and wriggled when Arnica was near, just because she was near, and it jumped and wriggled when she went away, waiting for her to come back. What Poor Johnny's heart wanted was to have Arnica sitting on the edge of Johnny's bed all the time.

"This is all I need!" Poor Johnny chided his heart, as it skipped about. "I'm the most footloose and fancy-free person in the world, may I remind you? Here today, gone tomorrow. I whistle my own tune, see? And I don't give a fig about anyone."

Well, he could talk to his heart till he was blue in the face—it just went on wobbling around in his chest. Whether he liked it or not, Poor Johnny had to face the fact that he'd fallen in love with Arnica. Without her the world seemed faded, the forest seemed unfriendly, wandering had lost its charm, and he felt as if there were a roof of ice-cold glass curving overhead rather than the wide, blue sky.

"No more freedom for you, Johnny!" moaned Poor Johnny.

"So, he's no longer free because he's fallen in love with Arnica?"

"That's what Poor Johnny thinks."

"And why isn't he free any longer?"

"Because he can't saunter about anywhere he fancies any more. He has to look after Arnica. He's responsible for her."

"Why? If he felt like sauntering about, Arnica wouldn't stop him."

"I don't think she would. But think about it; what if Arnica was to fall ill, just when Poor Johnny was considering going for a saunter? Then he'd need to stay at home and nurse her, make her better, and give her tender loving care."

"But if Arnica was to fall ill, then Poor Johnny wouldn't feel like going for a saunter. All he'd want to do is stay at home and nurse her back to health with tender loving care, wouldn't he?"

"You've got something there."

"You see! Then Poor Johnny is still the most footloose and fancy-free person in the world."

"Let's give him a bit of time. Maybe in a little while he'll realise that for himself."

When Poor Johnny's leg was better, he danced a happy little jig in the middle of the room. He thanked Arnica for making him well again, then he blushed and said:

"Arnica, there's something I want to tell you."

Arnica blushed too, and stared down at her shoes.

"I love you," said Poor Johnny.

"I love you too," said Arnica.

They hugged and kissed and, hand in hand, ran to find King Tirunt.

Before they could say a word the king said, smiling, "I know what you two want. You want to get married. I give you my blessing, my children. But there's something I want you to do. I believe that you love each other, but I'll believe it even more if your love can stand the test of time. Johnny, you go off wandering, and in half a year, if you still love Arnica and want to marry her, come back. Arnica, you wait for him, and if, when he comes back in six months, you still want to be his wife, we'll have a wedding feast so huge that our merrymaking will be heard for miles around. What do you say?"

They weren't very happy about it of course, but they agreed to the plan.

CHAPTER FOUR

In which a wicked spell is cast, and Poor Johnny's
love, sad to say, wavers a teeny-weeny bit

P oor Johnny got started with his wandering, and Arnica got started with her waiting. But Poor Johnny didn't enjoy his wandering. He didn't whistle, either cheerfully or sorrowfully; the only thing he could think of was, "Arnica, Arnica, Arnica."

Arnica's days went by slowly too. She kept looking at the calendar, but those pesky days were in no hurry. They dawdled so, you'd have thought they were afraid to let the sun set. Little by little, however, the time did pass.

As the six months neared their end, Arnica couldn't stand it any more, and she said to King Tirunt, "Come on, Father, let's go and meet Johnny!"

"But the six months isn't up yet."

"He might have miscounted. He might be coming early," said Arnica hopefully.

So they set off on the road leading from the castle, and went a good long way, looking ahead all the time in case there should be a tiny dot in the distance, a dot which would get bigger and bigger until, all of a sudden, there would be Poor Johnny standing in front of them. They took great care, naturally, not to step onto land belonging to the Witch of a Hundred Faces, knowing that that could bring them great trouble.

Poor Johnny didn't come, however, and, sure enough, one or two tears rolled down Arnica's cheeks.

"He must have forgotten," she said.

"Now then, the six months aren't even up yet," remonstrated King Tirunt. "No need for tears!"

Then, after all the other days had come and gone, the long-awaited day arrived too. Arnica was so happy she was walking on air. She put on her most beautiful dress and went out with King Tirunt to meet Poor Johnny. But on this particular occasion, they weren't as careful as they usually were; in all the excitement and anticipation they failed to notice that they had stepped over the boundary of the witch's land.

"He should be coming by now," said Arnica.

Just at that moment, right next to them, a bush rustled and out popped the Witch of a Hundred Faces.

"Waiting for Poor Johnny, are you?" she screeched. "Well, you'll have a long wait then! Poor Johnny is mine. Odds bodkins, turn into ducks this minute, both of you!"

There was a sizzling, a rumbling, a cracking, and—lo and behold!—two ducks appeared waddling about by the witch's feet. Arnica and King Tirunt. That's right, they had been turned into ducks.

Well, what could they do now? They toddled quickly back home, wobbling along in the way ducks do, and the sound of the witch's cackling followed them, triumphant and shrill. Arnica and King Tirunt got home, but when they arrived, all they could do was quack in astonishment. Where their castle with its thirty-six towers and three hundred windows had been, there was a tumbledown duck house, and there was no trace of the courtiers or the palace staff. Unless... Of course! That group of ducks over there on the round lake paddling to and fro, quacking and splashing; the palace staff and courtiers had been turned into ducks too, every one.

"Now then, what *do* we look like," said King Tirunt. "Now I'm the duck king, and you're the duck princess."

"Never fear," Arnica told him. "Poor Johnny will set us free in no time."

With that, she flopped into the lake and paddled sadly once round it, while the other ducks bowed their heads before her. For Arnica, even in the shape of a duck, was clearly a princess.

"Will Poor Johnny be able to set them free?"

"I hope so."

"But if he hasn't got any magic powers, how can he?"

"With his love. If he loves Arnica a great deal, he'll be able to set them free."

"Is love like magic then?"

"Yes, it is."

"But only in stories, right?"

"No. Not only in stories. In real life too."

Meanwhile, Poor Johnny was striding on eagerly.

"Whoopee!" he sang merrily. "The six months is up and you're my own, little Arnica!"

He hurried on as fast as his legs would carry him and entered the great wood, which belonged to the Witch of a Hundred Faces.

"I'll be there any minute now," he thought. He had worked up quite a thirst.

"There's bound to be a spring or a house hereabouts where I can ask for a glass of water."

No sooner had this crossed his mind, than he spotted a lovely little house beyond a bend in the road. It shimmered and shone in the sunshine; in the garden there were palm trees and eucalyptus trees, and in the centre of the garden, crystal clear water fell tinkling from a fountain.

"Now," thought Poor Johnny, "here's the place to ask for a glass of water."

He stood by the gate and called out, "Hello? Anyone home?"

The door of the house opened and out stepped a girl so adorably beautiful that Johnny's mouth fell open in astonishment. The beautiful girl smiled as kindly as she could manage.

"How can I help you, handsome traveller?" she asked.

"I... I'm really thirsty," stammered Poor Johnny, not able to take his eyes off the astonishingly beautiful girl.

"Come further in and sit by me," said the girl.

Poor Johnny sat himself in a basketwork chair, and the girl set down glasses of delicious ice-cooled fruit cordial, cuts of roast beef and snowy-white bread.

"I'm so glad you came by my house," said the lovely girl.

"Why?" asked Poor Johnny.

"Oh, I've known you for a long time," answered the girl. "You're Poor Johnny."

"How do you know me?"

"I saw you, when you were at King Tirunt's castle. And, and... you won't mind if I tell you?"

"What?"

"I fell deeply in love with you. It was love at first sight," said the girl, lowering her eyes.

"I'm sorry, miss, you being so beautiful and all," said Poor Johnny, "but I'm engaged to be married to King Tirunt's daughter Arnica. I'm heading there right now."

"Then I'm sorry for you, Poor Johnny," said the girl, "because while you were away, Arnica completely forgot about you."

"That can't be true!" cried Poor Johnny, dismayed.

"I'm afraid it is. She's married a prince, and has forgotten you even exist."

Johnny turned white as a sheet, and his heart began banging about alarmingly.

"I don't believe you," he said.

"Well, if you don't believe me, see for yourself. The castle's been knocked down, and they've moved away from the lake. You'll never find them."

Poor Johnny was sitting folded into the depths of the basket-work chair like a frail old man. His limbs had become so heavy, he thought he'd never be able to move them again.

"But she's lying! Not a word of it is true."

"Of course she's lying."

"Because she's... she's the Witch of a Hundred Faces?"

"Of course."

"But he's falling into her trap! You mustn't let him!"

"It's not up to me. Poor Johnny has to get out of it himself."

"And does he?"

"We'll see."

The beautiful girl's eyes, that is to say the witch's eyes, lit up.

"Now you'll be mine from top to toe," she thought. "You can't get away now! Odds bodkins!"

"Don't you worry yourself about Arnica," she cooed. "Stay with me. I'll be a more faithful wife to you than anyone else could. You'll be happy here, you'll see."

Poor Johnny was gazing and gazing at the girl, and very nearly reaching out his hand to stroke her. Then, in his mind's eye, he saw Arnica's sweet innocent face, and he snatched back his hand.

"It's not true. Arnica can't have left me!"

He leapt up, realising with amazement that wickedness was streaming towards him from the beautiful girl's eyes. Not stopping to think about it, however, he set off at a run. The Witch of a Hundred Faces once again transformed herself into a storm; lightning struck all around, a wind blew up.

"Now, wouldn't you know?" thought Poor Johnny as he dashed along, "I've ended up in the clutches of the very same witch as last time and oh! she almost had me convinced that Arnica had left me—what a nincompoop I am!" And he ran on as fast as he could. The witch tried the same wolf-howling and the same tree-stump-trick on him as before, but this time Johnny was on his guard. He skipped over the tree stump and was off the witch's land in two ticks.

But what was this? The palace had gone. There was only a sorry-looking duck house on the lakeshore, and some ducks paddling about on the water. But he didn't think for a moment that the witch might have been telling the truth after all. He knew well enough that this must be the result of some sort of spell.

"I'll find my Arnica," he thought, "if I have to walk to the ends of the earth to do it!"

Very despondent, he sat down on the shore and began to consider what to do. Well, as he was sitting there, he saw that there was a great commotion among the ducks on the water. They were flapping their wings and quacking loudly, and look! A lovely white duck was swimming straight towards Poor Johnny, coming out of the water, laying her head on Poor Johnny's knee and gazing and gazing at him with a sad look in her eye. Poor Johnny looked back sadly at the duck, stroked it and said:

"Hey, little duck, you haven't seen my sweet Arnica, have you?"

And as he said those words, the earth shook, a rumbling ran the length of the countryside, and in a flash, standing in its usual spot, was the palace with all its thirty-six towers and three hundred windows and the ducks had all changed back into people. "Help! Help!" came the voice of the Royal Chief Counter from the middle of the lake, for he couldn't swim, but luckily, the others were coming to his aid.

Arnica, too, had changed back and was probably even more beautiful than she'd been before. King Tirunt was also himself again. Their joy knew no bounds, until Arnica suddenly shrieked:

"Oh no, Johnny! Johnny, what's happened to you?!"

Indeed, something very strange was going on. At the very moment when the bewitched people had returned to their original shape, Poor Johnny had turned into a duck. Everyone stared in sorrow and wonder.

Oh dear, oh dear! There was something very amiss here. The chief royal brainboxes and the minor royal brainboxes put their heads together, as did the chief royal dunces and the minor royal dunces, and tried to decide what should be done, but they couldn't come up with anything. All they could be sure of, was that Poor Johnny had arrived, set them free from the spell they'd been under, and, in return, had ended up being a duck himself. But then, we knew that already.

As she stroked the duck, Poor Arnica wept, her tears falling heavy and fast like raindrops in a thundery shower, and she found herself saying:

"I don't want to be human if this is the price that has to be paid. I'd rather stay as a duck, if it means Johnny can be human again."

Well, in the blink of an eye, her wish came true. Johnny became a man, Arnica a duck.

"Oh no you don't!" shouted Poor Johnny. "After all, I'm the one in the wrong here. I should be the duck, and you should be a person."

And, as he said the words, that's precisely what happened; Johnny turned into a duck, and Arnica back into a girl. The palace staff couldn't make head nor tail of it—what was going on? What kind of cursed spell could this be?

"It looks like we've managed to mess something up here," said King Tirunt regretfully.

"It was me," said Poor Johnny, "I believed the witch, just for a moment. I almost agreed to stay with her, having got it into my stupid head that Arnica wanted to leave me. I let my love waver a teeny-weeny bit. I deserve this fate. I ought to be a duck for ever and ever."

"No way!" said Arnica. "I'd rather be the duck for ever and ever."

"Come now," said the Chief Courtier, "no need to get so upset about it. You can be the duck one day, and Johnny can be the duck the next day. You could go on like that quite happily till the end of the world."

"But if Johnny's a duck, then I want to be a duck too," said Arnica. "I want to be whatever he is."

The palace staff whispered among themselves, racking their brains, but couldn't come up with anything sensible to suggest.

"And what if Poor Johnny hadn't believed the witch when she was wearing her beautiful face, not even for one second? Then neither of them would have to be a duck now, would they?"

"In that case, no, they wouldn't."

"Can't anyone help them?"

"I don't know."

"You know what I think? I think they should go to the Seven-Headed Fairy and ask her to free them from the spell. She's a good fairy, the most kind-hearted in the world, so she's sure to do it. Don't you think?"

"But they don't know where the Seven-Headed Fairy lives."

"Then they should start looking!"

CHAPTER FIVE

In which it becomes clear that Tig-Tag,
the notorious thief, is blessed with great ball control

As luck would have it, there was among the courtiers an old woman who knew about the Seven-Headed Fairy.

"You know what?" she said to Arnica. "You should go and see the Seven-Headed Fairy. If anyone can help you, she can."

"Where does she live?" asked Arnica.

"That I don't know, to be sure," said the old woman.

"No problem. We'll find her," said Johnny. "Even if she lives at the ends of the earth, we'll find her."

Not wanting a big send-off, they quickly said their goodbyes to King Tirunt, the Chief Courtier, the Chief Royal Counter, to all the courtiers and palace staff, young and old, and set out on their journey.

"The good thing is, we can travel day and night," said Arnica.

"What do you mean, day and night?" said Poor Johnny, much surprised. "We'll need to sleep sometime."

"Oh, don't worry, we will," said Arnica. "From morning to night, I'll be the person and you'll be the duck. I'll tuck you under my arm and while I'm carrying you along, you can sleep just as much as you want. In the evening, we'll swap; you tuck me under your arm and carry me till morning. Meanwhile, it'll be my turn to sleep. That way we won't waste a single minute. We'll soon find the Seven-Headed Fairy, you'll see."

Poor Johnny was delighted to have such a clever bride, and, as it was getting dark just then, he became the person and Arnica the duck. Poor Johnny tucked her under his arm and set off. This time, however, he had enough sense to give the witch's land a wide berth.

They went on without stopping for seven days and seven nights and didn't meet a soul.

"Arnica, do you think we're going the right way?" said Poor Johnny, worried.

"Don't you worry, Johnny," said Arnica. "If we really want to find the Seven-Headed Fairy, we will."

"They do really want to, don't they?"

"Yes, they do."

"And if someone really wants something, does that mean they can do it?"

"I think so."

"You don't sound very sure."

"Well, I don't really know... I'm only sure that you have to really want it."

They were walking along the banks of a river—it was daytime, so Arnica was carrying Johnny—when they spotted a flock of sheep in the distance.

"Look! There's a flock of sheep over there," said Arnica. "That means there must be a shepherd, and he might be able to set us on the right track."

They found the shepherd stretched out in the cool shade of a tree.

"Never heard of any Seven-Headed Fairy," he said, shaking his head. "But I will give you a piece of advice. If you value your life, young miss, don't go any further."

"Why ever not?" asked Arnica.

"Because Tig-Tag, the notorious robber, is rampaging around this area," said the shepherd. "He'll steal your duck, and kidnap you too. You'd do better to turn back."

"The fact is, dear brother," said Arnica, "that I couldn't turn back, even if a hundred Tig-Tags were rampaging in the area."

And on she went.

"You're a brave lass, a brave one," murmured the shepherd. "I just hope you don't live to regret it."

Arnica did seem brave as she strode on with her duck, which was, as we know, none other than Poor Johnny. There was now, however, a tiny dark shadow in the centre of her heart. That shadow was fear: oh, she did hope she wouldn't bump into that fearsome robber, that Tig-Tag!

Sure enough, they'd walked on no more than half a fairytale mile, when a bush behind them rustled. Arnica spun round, thinking, "Oh no! Who's that?", and a grim-looking man with a moustache jumped out from behind the bush.

"Your money or your life!" he said, in bloodcurdling tones.

"Oh, goodness! You must be Tig-Tag, the notorious robber," said Arnica, because of course she knew at once who she was dealing with. "Have pity on me! I've got nothing to give you, not even a crooked sixpence."

"But you have got a duck," said Tig-Tag. "Your duck or your life!"

He was already stepping forward to take the duck from Arnica.

"Then I'd rather you took my life," said Arnica, very determinedly, and hid Poor Johnny behind her back.

Tig-Tag, the notorious robber, began to guffaw.

"Arguing with me, are you?" he guffawed. "All I'd have to do is blow on you, and you'd float off like the seeds on a dandelion clock."

"Arnica," whispered Poor Johnny. "Let's swap."

So Arnica said, "Let me be the duck, and Poor Johnny the person." And, just like that, they were.

56

Tig-Tag, the notorious robber, had reached out his hand towards Arnica, and was just about to grab her, when, to his utter amazement, he found himself face to face with a well-built, muscly young man. His jaw dropped, as you can imagine. But he shouted out anyway:

"Hand that duck over!"

At that, Poor Johnny gave Tig-Tag, the notorious robber, such a clout that he saw stars.

"My stars!" he exclaimed. Well, I did say he saw stars.

"This just stopped being funny," he thought and took to his heels. When he got to a safe distance, he shouted back to them, "You'll be sorry for this! I'll get my gang together and sort you out good and proper."

Johnny walked off hastily, breaking into a run from time to time.

"Until we're out of Tig-Tag's territory, I'll stay a person and you stay a duck," he said to Arnica. "I can probably handle them better."

Could he though? It was getting towards evening, when they began to hear whistling, cries of "Hulloo!" and the snapping of branches. The robbers were coming.

"There he is!" yelled Tig-Tag. "Head him off!"

They surrounded Poor Johnny, and though he fought back manfully, he didn't stand a chance against thirteen robbers. They tied him up, carried him off to their hideout, and threw him in a great iron cage along with his duck. When they had done a victory dance around the cage, Tig-Tag, the notorious robber, said, "Now you can just lie here till morning. By then we'll have thought of a nice little punishment for you."

"And we'll have duck stew for breakfast," added the gang's second in command.

The robbers quietened down, and then went to bed. Only Poor Johnny was left awake. This was it, they were going to be murdered by robbers. That it should come to this! Arnica couldn't sleep either, but instead of bemoaning their fate, her mind was whirring away.

"Johnny," she whispered.

"Yes?"

"Let's escape."

"From this iron cage? Fat chance!" said Johnny dismissively.

But Arnica knew what she needed to do. Up she got, and squeezed herself through the bars. It wasn't difficult. She was, after all, a duck. Then Poor Johnny saw what she was up to.

"Oh, you're a clever one, Arnica!" he thought.

He said the magic words; Arnica turned into a person, Johnny into a duck. All he had to do then was squeeze through the bars himself, and away they could go.

"You see, Johnny," said Arnica. "Every cloud has a silver lining."

"Really? Does every cloud have a silver lining?"

"That's what they say."

"So does it, or doesn't it?"

"Something good often does come out of something bad, but there are things that are just bad through and through."

"And if I cut my finger, for example. What's good about that?"

"What's good about that is, that you learn to be more careful when you're handling a knife, and you learn what it is to feel pain."

"And what about Mr Vincent from next door dying? What's good about that?"

"There's nothing good about that at all. That's just bad through and through."

Johnny had changed back into a person and was hurrying along as fast as his legs could carry him. But around dawn the robbers had realised that the cage was empty and had run off, lickety-split, to hunt down Poor Johnny. By midday they were hot on his trail, and then, all of a sudden, they'd caught up with him. At that moment, Poor Johnny happened to be in the middle of a melon field, and, for want of a better idea, he started to fling the melons at Tig-Tag and his gang. And would you believe it? Those robbers caught the melons so skilfully that not a single one got smashed. As the melons flew through the air, the robbers took control of them using their heads and feet just like the best footballers do with the ball on the pitch.

Poor Johnny gaped at them. The robbers, however, called out encouragingly, "Throw some more. It's a great game, this!"

"Well I never!" said Poor Johnny. "You lads have got amazing ball control!"

"What have we got?" asked Tig-Tag, the notorious robber.

"Ball control," repeated Poor Johnny. "You'd make a great football team."

The robbers just stared at him. Football? What was that?

Poor Johnny cobbled together a kind of rag-ball, and taught the robbers the rules of the game.

"What do you mean, we're not allowed to touch the ball with our hands?" blustered Tig-Tag, the notorious robber. "I'm allowed to do anything!"

"You may be allowed to do other things," Poor Johnny explained to him, "but touching the ball with your hands is forbidden in football, because it means the other side get a free kick."

In the end, even Tig-Tag understood that you can't have a game without rules, and resigned himself to the fact that not even he was allowed to touch the ball with his hands. And once he was playing, it didn't bother him, as he realised that he could manoeuvre the ball with his feet just as well as he wanted. The robbers all started to get into it, and were really enjoying themselves. Hardly surprising, given that they'd never played football in their lives, and were now learning what fun it is. It was a long time before they were tired of it, and then Tig-Tag beckoned Johnny over to him.

"Well, that's all great and everything, but we can't make a living out of it," he said. "We'll finish you off, and then get down to some robbing, ransacking, burgling and highway robbery."

"What do you mean, you can't make a living from football? You could make a living and then some!" said Poor Johnny.

"From what? From this game?" Tig-Tag was sceptical.

"Absolutely. I'm telling you, you lot play so well, you could beat any team in the world."

"OK, but where does that get us?" argued Tig-Tag, the notorious robber. "We win game after game, but what do we live off?"

"You'll be living the high life," said Johnny. "You'll get piles of money for playing."

"Pull the other one," said Tig-Tag, the notorious robber.

Poor Johnny wouldn't be put off. He kept on explaining until they began to twig that he was right.

"You just have a good wash and shave, and get some more respectable clothes on, and leave the rest to me," Poor Johnny told them.

The robbers squeezed themselves into their top hats and tails and marched into the nearest town with Johnny.

"This is my football team," Johnny told the townspeople. "They can beat any team you name."

"Come now," smiled the townspeople. "Don't you know that our town's team is World Famous FC? They'd get a dozen goals past your rabble, soon as look at them."

"OK. I bet you a thousand gold pieces my team wins," said Poor Johnny.

"You're on," said the townspeople.

"Oh dear," said Arnica. "Where are you going to get a thousand gold pieces from if Tig-Tag and his team get beaten?"

"Don't worry," said Poor Johnny, "our boys have talent coming out of their ears."

"But they're not in training," Arnica argued.

Poor Johnny smiled. "Not in training? They've been running from the police forces of seven countries. They've had all the training they need in both long-distance running and sprinting. You'll see, they won't have any problems in that department."

The match was fixed for the following afternoon. The stadium was packed, the spectators crammed in like sardines. World Famous FC ran out onto the pitch, the players puffing out their chests. Those thousand gold coins were as good as theirs already. Tig-Tag

and his team ran out too. The Chief of Police was sitting in the stands. He narrowed his eyes as he looked down at Tig-Tag.

"That centre forward looks very familiar to me," he said to the Deputy Chief of Police.

"Looks familiar to me too," said the Deputy Chief of Police.

The match got under way. Well, World Famous FC had never seen the like! Without losing the ball once, the robbers powered ahead like an express train. The spectators gaped slack-jawed at Tig-Tag's expert sidesteps and feints. The notorious robber and his team won 9–0. Tig-Tag alone had five goals to his name. After the match, as the thousand gold pieces were counted into his hand, he couldn't believe his eyes.

"We never got this much, even from our best and biggest robberies," whispered Tig-Tag happily to Poor Johnny. "You won't catch us going back to crime after this!"

And that's how Tig-Tag, the notorious robber, became Tig-Tag, the notorious centre forward.

"Tell me, what's your name?" he asked Poor Johnny.

"Poor Johnny," said Poor Johnny.

"Great!" said Tig-Tag, the notorious centre forward. "We'll name our team after you, as an expression of our gratitude. From this day forward, we'll be known as Poor Johnny FC."

And that's what happened. When you've learned to read and you're looking through old, yellowed newspapers, you'll find that Poor Johnny FC beat every football team in the world and easily too; they won the European Cup, the World Cup, the Seven Seas Cup and they also won the Cup of Cups.

"If Tig-Tag and his men could play football so well, why did they become robbers? Why didn't they become footballers in the first place?"

"Because they didn't know that they could play football. Poor Johnny noticed how good they were and then he helped them."

"So people don't always know what they're good at?"

"Very often they don't, no. They spend their time doing something else, rather than what they have a talent for."

"But everyone does have a talent for something?"

"Yes, they do. Everybody."

"Really?"

"Really truly."

"What about me? What do I have a talent for?"

"That'll become clear as you get older."

"So there's no talent of mine becoming clear right now?"

"Oh, yes there is. You can ask very good questions."

"Then, what I'm asking now is, when will Arnica and Johnny finally find the Seven-Headed Fairy?"

"They can find her if you want, but then it would be the end of the story."

"Let's not have it be the end just yet, OK?"

"My thoughts exactly, because they've still got to meet Victor Coppermine."

"Who's Victor Coppermine?"

"He's a small, plump man with glasses. He lives in the middle of a great meadow full of flowers, and keeps watch to see if anyone is coming his way. But people generally give him a wide berth."

"Why, is he wicked?"

"There's not a wicked bone in his body. It's just that he takes offence at everything."

CHAPTER SIX

In which Victor Coppermine takes offence many times, but they get the better of him

P oor Johnny made his way along cheerfully, and Arnica, tucked under his arm, was cheerful too. They were happy that they had managed to arrange a better life for Tig-Tag and his gang.

"The countryside is getting prettier all the time," said Poor Johnny. "I'm sure the Seven-Headed Fairy lives somewhere near here."

"Yes, we must be nearly there," nodded Arnica. "Look at this lovely meadow. It's full of flowers."

The meadow was so lovely that just walking through it made you feel happy. All around, flowers were bobbing and swaying, their scent wafting in the breeze, and there were emerald-green lizards flickering through the grass.

"It's strange that there's no one else coming this way," said Poor Johnny. "I'd think just being in this place and breathing as much as you want of this wonderful smell would be sure to put anyone in a good mood."

Just at that moment there appeared, rising from out of the grass, first a mop of tousled hair, then a pair of black-rimmed glasses, and behind the black-rimmed glasses, a melancholy black-rimmed face.

"And what about me?" it said. "I don't count as a person then?"

"I beg your pardon," said Poor Johnny. "I didn't see you there."

The person with the tousled hair let out a cry of pain.

"Oh yes you did! You saw me when you were a long way off. You just didn't want to meet me, you wanted to avoid me!"

And there, in the corner of the person's eye, glistened a fat crocodile tear.

Poor Johnny could only gape at him.

"How could I be trying to avoid you? I don't even know who you are."

"That's right, pile it on! Go ahead, claim that you don't know who I am, that you don't know I'm Victor Coppermine, and that everyone goes out of their way to avoid me."

It made no difference what Poor Johnny said to him; Victor Coppermine just puffed and pouted and moaned and groaned and hung his large, tousled head. Oh boy, was he offended!

Johnny spent an hour trying to console him. He spent two more hours trying to console him—no luck. The truth is, Johnny could console Victor Coppermine all he liked, Victor Coppermine would still be inconsolable.

Unsurprisingly, Johnny got fed up with all this consoling. He moved aside and whispered to Arnica, "Let's leave this Victor Coppermine to it. We're just wasting our time. We'll never get to the Seven-Headed Fairy like this."

"Now then, Johnny, giving up already?" chided Arnica. "We can't leave him here all sad and sorrowful and moping and miserable. We've got to cheer him up."

They tried all day, but by evening he wasn't any more cheerful.

"Maybe by the morning he will have forgotten about being offended," thought Poor Johnny, and they lay down to sleep.

When the sun rose in the morning, it rose very cheerfully. The whole world was cheered at the sight of it.

"Maybe Victor Coppermine will feel more cheerful when he wakes up," thought Poor Johnny. This just showed how little he knew Victor Coppermine. For barely a moment after Victor Coppermine opened his eyes, there was Victor Coppermine's finger jabbing at Poor Johnny.

"You wanted to leave me here. You wanted to cut and run,"

accused Victor Coppermine, and was so offended all that day too, that Poor Johnny tried in vain to cheer him up from morning to night.

And so it went on, day after day. Poor Johnny didn't know what to do. "We'll never get to the Seven-Headed Fairy!" he sighed to himself.

Poor Johnny's hair even started to turn grey. First one hair, then two. And Victor Coppermine just crouched and grouched.

"What on earth are we going to do?" Johnny asked Arnica. Victor Coppermine's head shot up.

"Aha!" he said. "You'd rather talk to your duck. I knew it! I knew it! You think I'm a quacking good joke, don't you?"

And there he was, affronted all over again for a whole day. After one more night, Arnica whispered something to Poor Johnny.

"Do you think it'll help?" asked Poor Johnny. He looked haggard.

"Let's hope so," said Arnica fervently.

The next morning, when Victor Coppermine opened his eyes and wrinkled up his brow and thought, "Now what shall I take offence at today?" Poor Johnny beat him to it.

"Aha!" said Poor Johnny. "I see you scowling at us. You're fed up that I'm still here with my duck. You can hardly wait till we're gone."

He gave Victor Coppermine a hurt look.

Well, Victor Coppermine had never been in such a tricky situation. Someone had actually taken offence before he could.

"No, really," he explained. "I'm sorry. I didn't mean to scowl at you. I truly am glad that you're here and glad that your duck is here too."

"A likely story! No need to explain. I can see you hate us."

Well, poor Victor Coppermine just fell to pieces. He'd never experienced anything so awful. He was not the one offended;

someone else had taken offence at him. Dear oh dear! He looked agitatedly this way and that and tried to cheer Johnny up. He couldn't grasp what had happened.

"Johnny got the better of Victor Coppermine this time."
   "He certainly did."
   "Is there anyone we know who takes offence at the drop of a hat?"
   "There certainly is."
   "And why does that person take offence at the drop of a hat?"
   "Because he thinks the world revolves around him, that he's the only one who can be fed up, that he's the only one who can be having a difficult time. It's all him, him, him. It never occurs to him that other people have their troubles too."
   "But Victor Coppermine will realise that, won't he?"
   "Oh yes, he certainly will."
   "But Poor Johnny wasn't really offended, was he?"
   "Of course not. He only took offence in the interests of education."
   "And do you sometimes take offence in the interests of education?"
   "Yes, I do."
   "And do you ever take offence for real?"
   "Yes, I do, unfortunately."
   "So you think the world revolves around you, too?"
   "There are times when I do, of course. But you shouldn't forget that it is also possible to feel really offended."
   "And if we feel really offended, then it's all right to take offence?"
   "In that case, yes."
   "And when that happens you're not thinking that the world revolves around you?"
   "Not then, no."

"So the world doesn't revolve around me either?"

"Not you either."

"Then who does it revolve around?"

"No one... Or rather, everyone."

Victor Coppermine went on and on pleading with Poor Johnny, until at last Johnny very condescendingly agreed to forgive him.

"It's all right, Victor. I'm not cross any more," and, hastily, not wanting to give Victor Coppermine time to get offended again, he told him their story; how the Witch of a Hundred Faces had cast a spell on them, and how they were looking for the Seven-Headed Fairy.

"Well, why didn't you say so in the first place?" cried Victor Coppermine, rather shrilly.

"How could we, when you were always crouching and grouching like a bad-tempered turkey-cock?"

"I see your point," said Victor Coppermine, shaking his head. "I'm sorry. But, you see, I actually know where the Seven-Headed Fairy lives."

"Where?" Poor Johnny's heart jumped.

Victor Coppermine pointed into the distance.

"You see that shingle-roofed palace on the horizon?"

"Yes, I can make out something like a building."

"Well, that's King Ayahtan Kutarbani's palace. Behind it is where the Land of Wonders begins. That's where the Seven-Headed Fairy lives."

"Well, that's really kind of you to tell us. Thank you, Victor! You see how kind and clever you are when you're not taking offence."

"Are you saying I'm a kind and clever person?"

"Yes, I am, because it's true. Only when you're not offended of course."

"But, what can I do when people go out of their way to avoid me? When you get to the Seven-Headed Fairy, please ask her to help me."

"You don't need the Seven-Headed Fairy for that," said Poor Johnny. "Just don't take offence all the time. If someone looks at you with a sad face, don't stick your nose in the air. Ask them what's wrong. You never know, you might be able to help them."

"Me? Help them?"

"Why not? You've helped us, haven't you?"

Victor Coppermine gazed at them in amazement. His black-rimmed eyes were no longer dark, but shining. When Poor Johnny

and Arnica left him, he stood waving for a long time. Then he began to shout, "Hey, everyone! Everyone! Come to my meadow!"

The people were suspicious at first. "Watch out! Don't let him take offence at anything," they thought to themselves, but when they did in fact get closer and closer to him, and saw that he wasn't taking offence, they began to talk very happily with him. Victor Coppermine talked happily too, and even told a few jokes.

"Well!" they said to him. "Who'd have thought it? You really are quite a nice fellow!"

And Victor Coppermine's joyful shouting reached even Poor Johnny and Arnica.

"Well!" he was shouting. "Who'd have thought it?! I really am quite a nice fellow!"

CHAPTER SEVEN

In which Poor Johnny and Arnica meet the twelve very-much brothers and Arnica gives them a proper telling-off

P oor Johnny's heart was bursting with happiness, partly because Victor Coppermine was shouting so joyfully, and partly because in no time at all they'd be in the Land of Wonders, appearing before the Seven-Headed Fairy.

"But if they're heading to the Land of Wonders, then they'll be bound to meet the twelve brothers."

"Which twelve brothers?"

"You said once that there were twelve brothers living near the Land of Wonders."

"I said that?"

"Of course! Don't you remember? You said they were *very-much* brothers!"

"Ah, the very-much brothers! I know. Well, of course Poor Johnny and Arnica will be meeting them."

Poor Johnny and Arnica were perhaps halfway between Victor Coppermine's flowery meadow and Ayahtan Kutarbani's shingle-roofed palace, when they spied a little tumbledown thatched cottage.

"I'm really thirsty," said Arnica. "Let's ask here for a glass of water."

Poor Johnny went into the house, calling out a polite greeting as he did so, and saw that there were eleven grumpy-looking men sitting round a table. They looked so alike that it was clear they were brothers. Johnny was just about to ask for a glass of water, when all the eleven brothers cried out as if in pain, and each of them grabbed his own leg. The funny thing was that they all did it exactly at the same time, as if someone had ordered them to. Then all eleven of them proceeded to jump up from the table and hop about on their left legs, clutching their right legs as they did so.

"The idiot! The numbskull! The clumsy oaf!" they shouted.

"What's going on? Have you gone mad?" asked Poor Johnny, looking at them, astonished.

"Gone mad? Gone mad? Hang it all! It's that cack-handed clodpole—he's only gone and dropped the tree on his leg."

"Who has?"

"Our twelfth brother. He went off into the forest to cut wood and, bam! Ow, ow, how it hurts! He dropped the tree on his leg, the idiot."

"But how do you know?" asked Poor Johnny.

"There's a curse on us, didn't you know? If something hurts one of us, it hurts the rest of us too. Oh, oh, it's a horrible thing! Just imagine it, young man, just imagine how terrible our lives are. Not long ago this good for nothing fell into the river. He can't swim, so there he was in the water, struggling against the current and gasping for breath, and there we were all gasping for breath on the bank."

"Look who's talking! Yesterday you stuffed yourself silly and we all had a stomach ache all night! You greedy pig! Why do you have to eat so much?"

"Oh yes? You can talk! What about that time you got lost in the forest? We were starving and shivering for three days all because you never can be bothered to remember the way."

The eleven brothers were practically at each others' throats. Poor Johnny just stood looking from one to the other of them and shaking his head. Suddenly however, they left off squabbling and began to groan.

"Ooh, it's heavy!" they said.

"Ow, it's crushing my shoulder."

"Ugh, it's so prickly, this tree!"

"Hey, What's the halfwit doing, trying to carry such a weight?"

The eleven brothers grunted and groaned for all they were worth.

"Now what's the problem?" asked Poor Johnny.

"It's our twelfth brother, he's bringing the tree home, the one he dropped on his foot before... He must be mad, picking such a heavy one. Oh, what did we do to deserve this?"

Just then, Arnica spoke from under Poor Johnny's arm:

"You should be ashamed of yourselves!"

That made the brothers sit up and listen.

"Who said that? Did your duck just say something?"

"Is it a talking duck?"

"She's not really a duck. She's a princess," said Poor Johnny.

"Come on now! Pull the other one," said the brothers, grimacing and groaning and clutching at their shoulders. Apparently, their twelfth brother was really heaving the tree along.

"I can easily prove it," said Poor Johnny. "Let me be the duck, and Arnica the person!"

And, in a flash, there stood Arnica in front of the brothers holding the duck under her arm.

The eleven brothers' eyes grew wide as saucers.

"Cor, you're really beautiful," they said, disregarding the sour expression on Arnica's face.

"OK, so how does that work? Which one of you has to say that you should change over?" asked one of the brothers, while they all heaved a collective sigh of relief, the twelfth brother having put down the tree and stopped for a rest.

"Whichever one of us is the person, always," replied Arnica.

"And you don't worry that one day, when that one under your arm is the person, he might just toss you aside, and do a runner? You'd have to be a duck for ever then."

"Now you see? That's precisely the problem with you lot!" said Arnica angrily.

"Is it really true that, if one of them decided to do that, the other would have to stay a duck for ever?"

"Yes, it is."

"That hadn't even crossed my mind."

"I'm glad to hear it!"

"And Arnica and Poor Johnny? Has it crossed their minds?"

"Think about it. It would never cross their minds in a million years!"

"But you saw how it crossed the brothers' minds, didn't you?"

"Well, that's precisely why they're suffering so much. They've got a twisted way of thinking."

"If they didn't have such a twisted way of thinking, all the eleven brothers would go off to help the brother who's bringing the tree, wouldn't they? And then there'd be no need for all this moaning and groaning. If the twelve of them were to work together, it would be easier for all of them."

"There you go! That's just what Arnica wants to tell them."

"If the two of us became so very-much related that whatever hurt one of us hurt the other too, would that be good or bad?"

"I think that we are so very-much related. At least, what hurts you, hurts me too."

"But what I mean is, that if I fell flat on my face, you'd get bruises on your knees and your tummy."

"And would that be good or bad in your opinion?"

"If we were like that, I'd be really careful when I was running.

I'd make sure I didn't fall and get hurt because I wouldn't want it to hurt you too."

"That's very sweet of you."

"And you wouldn't smoke so much, would you? Otherwise I'd be coughing every morning."

"I think I'd give up smoking altogether."

"In that case, it wouldn't be so bad. We'd watch out for ourselves and each other too. Arnica should tell the brothers to look after each other, OK?"

"She's already telling them."

"Oh, you simpletons!" said Arnica. "When one of your brothers is in the river and can't swim, you'd rather gasp for breath on the bank than jump in and pull him out. And if another of your brothers is lost, you'd rather spend three days being hungry and cold than go out and look for him. What simpletons you are!"

"Yeah, right! If we did that we'd be at each other's beck and call the whole time," grumbled the brothers.

"But you could actually be the happiest people in the world," Arnica told them. "If one of you, no matter which brother he was, happened to fall in the river, he could be sure that the other eleven would jump in after him and pull him out. If one of you, no matter which brother he was, happened to get lost, he could be sure that the others would set off straight away to look for him. There could be so much trust and love in your hearts!"

"There's an idea!" said the oldest brother, and they all stared wide-eyed at Arnica. "Why didn't we think of it before?"

And, "Ugh!" all eleven of them grunted aloud. The twelfth brother had heaved the tree up onto his shoulder.

This time without hesitation, they leapt up and dashed off. They ran to the brother who was carrying the tree, and all eleven of them helped him with it. This way, with all twelve of them carrying it, the tree was almost no weight at all. No more need for grunting and groaning.

The twelve brothers were carrying the tree along very happily, when, all of a sudden, they started shouting, "Hey, our eyes are prickling. Which one of us is crying?"

"It's me. I'm crying," said the twelfth brother, "but it's because I'm so happy."

CHAPTER EIGHT

BEING ALSO THE LAST

*In which everything turns out all right and we get
to see the witch's hundred-and-first face*

Poor Johnny was delighted, Arnica too. Why wouldn't they be when the number of happy people in the world had just gone up by twelve? Well, before they knew it, they found themselves standing in front of Ayahtan Kutarbani's shingle-roofed palace. Ayahtan Kutarbani, who was looking out of the window, smiled and waved at them.

"The Seven-Headed Fairy's been expecting you!" he called to them cheerily.

"What? She knows we're coming?"

"Oh yes, she knows!"

Just then, they heard lovely faraway music, and they realised that the Seven-Headed Fairy was standing right there before them. She was looking at them kindly and smiling.

"Tell me then, what is it you would you like?" she asked.

"We'd like... we've come because..." stammered Poor Johnny, a little overawed. "We'd like to be whatever the other one is. Both of us ducks, or both of us people, whichever you want. Whichever we deserve... Please help us!"

The Seven-Headed Fairy made no reply, only smiled. Then, Poor Johnny discovered to his amazement that he was holding someone's hand. He was holding Arnica's hand, because they were both people now. They fell into each other's arms and were as delighted with each other, as only two people who are very, very much in love can be. The Seven-Headed Fairy's smile had shone into their hearts, and they knew that no evil spell would ever be able to touch them again.

"Did they say thank you to the Seven-Headed Fairy for helping them?"

"Of course they did. And now they're hurrying home to King Tirunt so that he can be happy too."

Arnica and Poor Johnny hurried home and they were so beautiful and so happy, that they cheered the hearts of everyone who saw them.

They spent one evening with the twelve brothers and one at Victor Coppermine's meadow which was full of flowers and merry noise. On the third they were in the town watching a big match just as Tig-Tag, the notorious centre forward, and his team won the Seven Seas Cup. By the fourth evening, they could make out the thirty-six towers of the palace that stood on the shores of the round lake.

"And what will become of the Witch of a Hundred Faces?"

"Why, what should become of her?"

"Do witches really exist?"

"No, they don't."

"But there's one in this story."

"You're the one who said there should be a witch in it. It wasn't my idea."

"But now I don't want there to be one in the story any more."

"She's going to lose her magic powers in any case, because this is the day that the seven years are up, remember?"

"She didn't manage to trap anyone into being her servant then?"

"No, she didn't."

"And what's she doing now?"

The Witch of a Hundred Faces was in front of her house, weeping and wailing.

"Oh, oh, I'm going to lose my magic powers. Oh, I've got less than an hour left, and then I'll have no power over anyone. Help me, just this once, grandmother of devils! Send someone this way, chase someone this way, sweep someone this way! Shh! What's that? Footsteps approaching. Someone's coming! Oh, grandmother of devils, you heard me! Thank you, thank you!"

She was all a-flutter with excitement, but when she saw who it was, her heart sank. For it was Arnica and Poor Johnny who were coming towards the witch's house. The kindly light of the Seven-Headed Fairy shone from inside them and the Witch of a Hundred Faces knew at once that she could have no hold over these two.

"You there, Poor Johnny!" she said angrily. "You've managed to ruin everything. The devil take your cursed freedom! You, you... Footloosest, fanciest, freest person in the world!"

"What's all this cursing, old mother?" said Poor Johnny. "Doesn't it get boring, always frightening people? Don't you tire of all this wickedness, this scheming, this double-dealing, this taunting, this flaunting, this yelling and howling? Did it never occur to you that you might eventually love someone? Or help someone?"

"Oh, you stupid, soft-hearted young man, you've become a slave to your feelings! Don't you know what fun it is gazing into terrified faces? Or what it feels like to be a storm tearing through a wood? Or to be a wolf howling? Or to be smoke twisting into the air? What do you know about it!"

"What a load of rubbish!" said Poor Johnny. "Has anyone ever loved you?"

"No," said the witch.

"And have you ever been in love?"

"No," said the witch.

"Well, there you are! You can have no idea how much more it's worth; no amount of flying around on broomsticks can compare to it."

"Are you serious?"

"Now's your last chance. In five minutes you'll lose your magic powers anyway. Free those poor people you lured into your power with your wicked treasure, and maybe you could still be a decent person."

"Oh, all right then," said the witch, somewhat alarmed. "Odds bodkins! Be free again!"

And lo and behold, all the people she had lured and enslaved began to emerge from the witch's cellar. They came out one by one, squinting in the light as the sunshine caressed their skin.

"Thank you, Poor Johnny," they said. "As for this one, she's going to get a good beating!"

And they all rushed at the Witch of a Hundred Faces.

"Oh no, dearest Johnny!" said the witch. "Don't let them hurt me!"

"I'm not going to let them. Just come here and stand behind me," said Poor Johnny, and he waved his hand at the people to show that they shouldn't hurt the witch.

Something popped in the witch's breast then, as if an iron band had broken and fallen off her heart, and she felt a kind of warmth deep inside, something she'd never felt before, something wonderful. Before she could help herself, the Witch of a Hundred Faces had stroked Johnny's arm. At that moment her magic powers left her and she became an ordinary old lady in a black headscarf.

"You won't send me away, will you? I can stay with you both, can't I?" she asked hopefully.

"Of course you can, Nana," Arnica told her. "You can stay with us."

"What do you think? If the Witch of a Hundred Faces hadn't been going to lose her magic powers anyway, would she still have been willing to be a proper old lady?"

"That's a tricky one. Quite possibly no."

"So she did it because she was forced to. That doesn't really count."

"Well, I don't know if it counts or not. All I can say is that once, later, when she was rocking little Johnny in her arms..."

"Did Arnica and Poor Johnny have a little boy?"

"Of course. So there she was bouncing little Johnny on her knee, and she said to him, 'You know, little Johnny, it was fun riding on a broomstick, it was fun flitting around as a bat, it wasn't bad being a storm and rushing through the forest either, but having you sitting here and smiling at me so lovingly and trustingly, well, I wouldn't exchange this for the world.'"

"Did she really mean it?"

"I think so, yes."

"And now it's the end of the story, isn't it?"

"Yes, it is."

"Everything turned out all right in this story."

"Is that a problem?"

"Not at all! That's what made it so good... Does everything turn out all right in real life?"

"In real life? No. Sadly, no."

"So this wasn't a true story then?"

"It was actually. What it's saying is that we, both of us, really, really want everything to turn out all right in real life."

"Yes, I do really, really want that. You said that the important thing is to really, really want something. Even if it won't necessarily succeed."

The End

PUSHKIN CHILDREN'S BOOKS

We created Pushkin Children's Books to share tales from different languages and cultures with younger readers, and to open the door to the wide, colourful worlds these stories offer.

From picture books and adventure stories to fairy tales and classics, and from fifty-year-old bestsellers to current huge successes abroad, the books on the Pushkin Children's list reflect the very best stories from around the world, for our most discerning readers of all: children.